MW00908851

The Parisian Mystery

By

Ariesta Angelis

Dedicated to:

My folks for showing me what I can do

My Kids for showing me who I wanted to be

My Grand-babies for showing me happiness and joy

My Love for believing in me and loving me always

Chapter 1

On a night during a violent, raging storm Jeanna was startled by a knocking at her apartment door. When she opened it there stood a tall, dark silhouette. Just as she managed to stammer out, "May I help you?" a bolt of lightning shot across the sky followed very quickly by an extremely loud clap of thunder. After she recovered from her initial shock, she noticed he was wearing a uniform from Special Delivery and holding a box.

He looked at her and in a gruff voice asked, "Are you Jeanna St. Claire?"

Taken aback by his tone she shakily said, "Yes, may I help you?"

"I have a delivery for you marked urgent. The boss told me to drop it off on my way home so here it is." He said with the gruffness still in his voice but added a very creepy attempt at a smile that looked much more like a sneer. "I need you to sign here." He said as he stabbed at the line on his handheld with the stylus.

"Th-thank you, I am sorry you had to come out on such a dreadful night." Jeanna stammered as she signed the device and then took the package. He grunted, turned and walked to his van. Jeanna hurried into her living room of her apartment and looked at the box. There was no return address and it was postmarked from Paris.

As she began to open the package another clap of thunder and bolt of lightning happened simultaneity outside. Inside the package there was a beautiful diamond ring at least 2 carats, a folding fan with a gorgeous picture of the Eiffel Tower at sunset, a beautifully sculpted glass train and a postcard from downtown Paris with Chez Jolie as the center piece. This part was odd because that was where he old boyfriend; Christian; was working. Jeanna was confused as to who on earth would send her a box, especially marked urgent, from Paris. Especially since she only knew two people in Paris. One was Christian, but they hadn't spoken, in about six months, since she told him what a jerk he was being moving there to learn about cooking because his parents wanted him to go into the restaurant business with them. Seriously she had a point he wasn't cut out for it, for crying out loud he could burn water. The other person was her Mom and they hadn't parted on the greatest terms either. She hadn't talked to her in about the same time.

Jeanna began pacing her studio apartment, as she passed the full-length mirror on the far wall, she stared at it without seeing the reflection of her own tall athletically built frame and long wavy auburn hair. She only saw her own gray colored eyes as she thought about Christian and their last visit together. He had told her he was going to study culinary arts in France to make his family happy. She just stared at him with those eyes and tried to read his real emotions and reasoning; she could usually do that with anyone; but as usual she couldn't read him. She had yelled at him and told him what a fool he was for going. He had such a great sleuthing mind and they could really make a go of being investigators. They had solved so many "cases" as kids. Granted they were things like missing bikes, cats, homework assignments or jewelry, but they were really good at it. As they had gotten older, they had even helped with bigger things that the police didn't really seem interested in or that people didn't want to bother the police with. Plus, she knew if they could get the proper training, they could be even better investigators.

Jeanna had to admit she never told Christian the real reason she was so upset. She had never had a real boyfriend, until he had asked her to go out during their Junior year. Mostly they had begun dating because the other kids had gotten so used to seeing them together, they all just assumed they were dating. Her parents used to say they were attached at the head, because every time Jeanna and Christian were together they were absorbed in paper looking for some kind of mystery to solve or reading a mystery book. Sometimes they even went as far as to create their own mysteries for each other to solve.

That was when it hit Jeanna, maybe Christian had decided to forgive her and had sent her a mystery to solve. If so, why send it anonymously though? Was he having fun or was he in trouble? She had kept tabs on his restaurant in Paris and had seen there had been some trouble there. Did he possibly need her help? It had been a bit since she had looked up the restaurant, so she ran to her laptop and did a search for any news about it. What she saw horrified her.

She called Charlie; the evening news guy she had befriended a few years ago when she had been interviewed for and article about her mother. He told her that it was true and that they had a suspect in custody for it.

Jeanna thanked him and immediately grabbed her cell phone and sent a text to her friend JB and told him she needed a flight to Paris the next morning. He called her immediately and she told him the whole story as she knew it. JB; was one of her father's oldest friends and he had a charter business that had a Concorde plane he used to take high class clients wherever they wanted to go. Many just used it to go to and from the city when they wanted to get away to the country as they called it. JB promised he would meet her at the airfield as soon as the sun was up and they both hoped for clear skies. She thanked him and looked back at the screen on her laptop. She almost wanted to cry. She had to get there soon, and she hoped her suspicion wasn't right about who had been arrested.

Chapter 2

Jeanna went to her room pulled out her small suitcase threw in some jeans, a few t-shirts, underclothes and one pair of PJs. She grabbed her passport from her small safe and her PI credentials she had worked so hard for. She also grabbed her backpack for her laptop and her trusty sleuthing kit, then went back into the living room to read the article more closely. She couldn't believe that Christian's restaurant had been burned and she feared that he was being held as a suspect.

Jeanna's next call was to Christian's mom. She may have been upset with her for pushing him to go into the family business, and how she had treated her, but she also knew how much that woman loved her son. After an hour of promising to let her know as soon as she found out anything Jeanna hung up. Her next call wasn't going to be as fun.

Her mom picked up on the third ring and asked groggily, "Jeanna what is wrong? Why are you calling so late? Are you okay?" Jeanna had forgotten the time difference over there.

"Mom I'm sorry. I wanted to let you know I was going to be coming to Paris tomorrow." Jeanna hated to admit she may need her help; especially after how they had parted.

"Really..." Her Mom said now more awake.

"You've read the papers, there right?" Her silence said it all. "Well I'm coming to see if I can help and make sure he is okay."

"Jen you don't even know if he is in trouble yet."

"I do know mom, I have this terrible feeling he is, and I'm sure he asked me for help." She told her about the package she had just gotten and told her she had a flight over the next morning.

"Okay hunny, I'll leave your name at the gate and a pass for you at the front desk."

"Thank you, mom. And mom..." pausing to gather her composure.

"I know hun. I love you too and I understand."

Jeanna didn't sleep well at all, she was tossing and turning all night long. She finally gave up, got up and headed to the air field, she was waiting when JB got there. She looked exhausted and of course JB told

her so. She smiled and thanked him, laughing a little. He told her the

plane was in the hanger, to go ahead and climb aboard. He had to check

on the flight plan he had faxed last night and see if his co-pilot had shown

up.

Jeanna climbed on the plane and remembered all the times her and

her mom had flown on it back and forth to DC for her job. She began

thinking of the weekend Christian and she had flown down to see her

mom before he left for Paris. Her mom had told Jeanna it was a great

opportunity for Christian and she was being selfish pressuring him to stay.

The weekend ended up being one night when Jeanna found out that her

mom had been offered a posting in Paris and that she was taking it. She

was hoping Jeanna would go with her. Jeanna had been so furious she told

them both to have a great life in Paris and ran from the apartment. She

flagged a cab and went to the airport catching JB as he was flying back

that night. She had just lost her dad that week and then she lost her

boyfriend and mom, it was more than even she could handle. That was

only 6 months ago, and it still hurt to remember how betrayed she had felt

by them both

Her dad had gotten sick and she had decided to stay home to take care of him when her Mom's job brought her to DC. Her dad had always told her that he had wanted her mom to go, but Jeanna felt her Mom had abandoned him anyway. She thought her mom should have been there to take care of him and to help her deal with all the emotions she was going through. Her mom understood her being upset with her. She had even offered to help her out, but Jeanna was too angry and stubborn to accept it.

Her dad had told her was going to get a live-in nurse and Jeanna had said no way she would take care of him, before she would have a stranger come in. He had developed a big word for cancer as well as losing his left leg. He had coped with the leg so well no-one even knew it was a prosthetic one. But when his cancer hit him his health and spirits took a serious nosedive.

Jeanna had been studying to be a detective then. She had dropped out of college to be home with him. She decided to skip the criminal justice side and just jump into what she really wanted to do. After all she had agreed to go to college just to please her folks. She had started taking PI courses online while took care of her dad.

Jeanna didn't have to worry about herself financially regardless of what she did; her dad's family had been one of the original settlers in the area. As the town had grown the family had decided to lease off some land or to just sell other pieces outright. To say that he was rich was an understatement, even his hospital bills were covered since his family not only leased the land to the hospital, but they paid to build it. They had even added the cancer center, so others didn't have to travel so far for their treatments.

Her mom's family wasn't hurting for money either, they had moved to the town as a getaway from the city. Her grandfather had been one of those unique politicians; one who figured after three terms he was ready to let fresh blood in and had taken an assignment to the diplomatic corps. Her mom had been in college in the states when he and her mom had gone on his first assignment overseas. She had gotten a call that they had been killed in a plane crash, returning to their post from a trip abroad.

Her mom had been studying Poli-Sci in hopes of running for office herself one day, instead she took her father's posting when they asked her. That was where she met Jeanna's dad, he was one of the servicemen that had been assigned to protect her. He was assigned to her as soon as she took over the post and he had actually told her she was way to outspoken and stubborn to make a good diplomat. Everyone expected him to end up kicked off the assignment in less than a month because he kept calling out her mistakes. Instead she fell in love with him, this was very uncommon and very frowned upon. After he lost his leg protecting her, she told her advisors to kiss off and they were married six months later. One year after that Jeanna came along.

Since her dad's military career had come to an abrupt end, he had become mister mom. Jeanna became his world and as much as her mom could she showered attention on her too. Despite her mom's attempt Jeanna became "Daddy's little princess" and always was, right up to his death six months ago. That is why it broke her heart so bad when her dad had passed away.

Her mom had come back for the funeral and Christian had tried to see her then as well. She had refused to see him and completely ignored her mom while she was in the house. Right after her dad passed and the services were over, she closed up the house and moved into a little studio apartment. She was haunted by the memories with every turn in the house, they were just too much for her to deal with at the time.

JB brought her back to the present as he climbed on board and said, "You ready to go?"

"Yes. And thanks again."

"It's the least I can do for my favorite PI." He said with a smile.

Chapter 3

In a Paris jail Christian was sitting waiting to find out what they were going to do with him. He had called Jeanna's mom as soon as they had come to arrest him in class. He had already sent the package to Jeanna hoping she would come to see him and help him find out what happened. Now he was hoping she could clear his name. He had no idea if she got the package, but he knew if she got the package, she would figure out he needed her. He just hoped she was willing to help him, they hadn't parted on the best terms. She wouldn't even talk to him at her Dad's funeral.

Christian couldn't blame her too much though, but how could he tell his parents no when they needed him to help with the restaurant, so they didn't lose it. He hadn't told Jeanna about that part of his reason, because he didn't want her to know how much financial trouble, they really were in. He didn't tell her he had gotten a scholarship because he was to proud and even a little ashamed.

He had wanted to stay and become a PI with her. They both loved mysteries and loved helping people, so it had seemed perfect for them to become PI's together. The problem was his parents really needed him and

he couldn't turn his back on them, no matter how much he wanted to be

with Jeanna. It was even worst because, as far as Jeanna knew he had no

idea how to cook, but he actually was a really good cook. He had just

been afraid to ever tell her or even show her because he figured she'd pick

on him.

What had hurt him the most though was that they had known each

other since preschool and in all that time he had been in love with her.

She was smart, funny and not afraid of anything. She had even, eventually

earned the respect of the local bullies by helping their leader prove he

hadn't vandalized the school statue. She was one of the most fair-minded

people he had ever met. She would give anyone the benefit of the doubt

even if everyone else thought they were a bad element. That's why it blew

him away when she got so angry at him for telling her he was going to

Paris to study. She told him he was the densest guy she had ever met and

that he had no clue about anything. Those were pretty harsh words and he

had taken them to heart when he left.

Now he knew she was right about him being dense though. He

finally realized how much she had loved him and that he had been blind to not see that and the fact that he had never told her how much he truly

loved her was the most upsetting thing to him. He could only hope he

would finally get the chance. He laid back on his bunk, stared at the

ceiling hoping she had gotten the package and praying she understood it.

But most of all hoping she would be willing to come and help him.

Because maybe that would mean she still loved him.

Chapter 4

Jeanna was just touching down in Paris at the small airfield JB's friend owned when he said, "I'll take these to your mom for you and I'll get myself checked into the hotel."

"No, you won't mom has made arrangements for us both to stay with her. Just let them know at the gate who you are and that you brought me over. Tell mom I went to see Christian. And JB," He turned, "thanks again."

"No thank you. I was looking for an excuse to get away. Tell Christian I said hi and to keep his chin up."

"I will, be careful JB." she called as she rushed out to catch a cab to take her to the police station Christian was being held.

About twenty minutes later her cab pulled up in front of the police station, she got out, paid him and headed up the steps. When she got to the front desk she spoke in French to the Sargent and asked to speak to Christian. The man at the desk looked at her and asked who she was and how she was related to him. She told him her name and pulled on the ring,

putting it on her finger, preparing to tell him she was Christian's fiancée.

The man at the desk looked at his book in front of him and said,

"You are on the list to see him. It says here you are attached to Embassy."

She smiled, gotta love her mom. "Yes. I am one of the junior

assistances to the ambassador. She wants to get all the information she

can and for me to find a lawyer for him."

"Fine, follow me." He grabbed the keys and what looked like a

fax and headed to the back area of cells.

"Again gotta love mom" Jeanna admitted to herself

As they walked down the aisle Jeanna felt uncomfortable as the

guys in the cells leered at her and catcalled in French, unfortunately she

spoke it fluent enough to know what they were suggesting. Her face was

flushed as she got to Christian's cell. When she looked in and saw him

laying on his cot she almost cried.

He looked up and was shocked, "Jeanna I am so glad you are here? I see you got my package." She saw him looking at the ring she was wearing and self-consciously began playing with it.

"So, it was you who sent it to me. I thought it was and then I heard about what happened and I came to see if I can help."

"Well if you can get me out of here that would be a great help."

"Oh, I'll see what I can do. Mom has faxed ahead a form, so we'll see what can be done." Jeanna said as she looked at the guard and the paper he had from her mother. She noticed it stated that Christian was to be released into the custody of the Jeanna to bring him to the embassy.

The guard read the paper and looked at Jeanna and said, "You have to give me a few moments to talk to my superiors and verify this."

"Of course. May I stay here with Christian until you return?"

"Yes, but you have to stay outside of the cell," He said as he pulled up a chair for her to sit on. "This could take a while." He walked away and Jeanna sat down on the chair and looked at Christian.

"So, tell me what happened?" Jeanna said taking out here tablet to jot notes on.

"Still the detective huh, and all business, okay here goes." and Christian relayed what he knew about the fire and his side of the story. He said he had been having issues with one of the other students in the class, who had also gotten an internship at the Chez Jolie. Christian was telling her how he had gotten so much better at cooking and he was learning a whole lot from Monsieur Jolie. He confessed he still liked to solve mysteries and that they had one at the restaurant. The owner couldn't explain the missing inventory and he had heard about how the two of them had helped to solve some mysteries in the states. Since he didn't want to involve the police, he had asked Christian to investigate it for him. That was why Christian had been at the restaurant so late.

Christian had finally figured out what had happened to the supplies, but before he could tell the owner the fire had happened and almost all the evidence was burned up. All he had was the flash drive he had hidden in his apartment. He smiled at her and asked, "Your turn? What really brought you here?"

Jeanna looked at him and said, "You have evidence in your apartment? Why didn't you tell the police?"

"Ah... Avoiding my question I see. I guess I see how this is going to go. And yes, I do. As I said my boss didn't want them involved until I talked to him. I was going to talk to him after class when I was arrested. Now are you going to answer my question?"

Jeanna looked at him and said, "I already did. I heard you were in trouble and I wanted to help." He just looked at her with that knowing look and nodded at her hand. She twirled the ring again and said, "OK fine. When I got that weird package it the mail, I couldn't resist I did some research and that's when I heard about what happened, so I came here to make sure you were safe."

"So, you do still have feelings for me?" He said with a smug smile.

"Stop gloating! You were the one who left me and came here."

"Are we going to have this argument again? We know you still have feelings for me and that I have feelings for you, even if you don't believe me, so why are we fighting them."

"Cause you are an insufferable jackass, who has to always be right." This got her a snort and another knowing look. "And I didn't say I was fighting my feelings for you. I still have them because we've known each other since preschool, and that kind of stuff is hard to let go. But you are so conceited, you just don't get it." Jeanna stood up so quickly she knocked over the chair. "I am going to see what is holding this up, so I can drop you off to the embassy and then try to help solve this arson, so I can go home and get on with my life again."

"Oh yeah that's right run away from your feelings again, and from me." She turned on him. "Okay so I was the one who left, but you haven't talked to me since I left. You should also remember this isn't the small town we grew up in, this is another country and they don't like outsiders meddling in their business."

"Oh, just shut up. At least let me get the flash drive to your boss for you, tell the guard to give me your keys, so I can get that and some clean clothes for you."

"Fine, but you are still running away." Jeanna just stared at him and finally stuck out her tongue at him. He tried to hide a grin and said, "It's hidden in a place you should be able to find easily. Let me just say it's hidden with my heart."

Jeanna smirked back and said, "By the way I'm not running away." She started walking and turned and said, "I'm walking away briskly." She also added, "And you know I hate it when you are so cryptic." She turned back around and headed to the front of the cell area to call for the guard.

Chapter 5

At the main cell doors she called for the guard, he opened the door and she told him that Christian wanted her to get him some clean clothes from his apartment. The guard told her that his Inspector wanted to see her in his office. She said fine and asked for directions to the office. He walked her there and knocked on the door to let his Inspector know she was there.

"Entrez Madamesoille." Jeanna walked in and the Inspector pointed to the chair in front of his desk as he spoke quickly on the phone in French to someone. She took the seat and waited. He hung up the phone with a bit more force than she felt necessary. "Madamesoille, why are you here and what is your connection to the embassy?"

"Monsieur I am here at the request of the Ambassador. I am her daughter and we both know your suspect. We want him to be at the embassy until his trial. We fear he could be in danger; since the Chez Jolie was a landmark; there may be some who are unforgiving and maybe even hostile about it."

"Madamesoille, we would never allow our personal feelings to prevent us from protecting him. I am highly offended by this."

"We weren't meaning you or your officers, and I didn't mean to offend you Inspector. We just want to prevent anything from happening to him, I know you can appreciate our concern. We trust you will do all you can to protect him, but why make things more complicated for you and your men when we can just keep him at the embassy. If it would make you feel better you can post a man there and retain his passport. "

He looked at Jeanna skeptically and said, " Like I have the man power for that and if we retain his passport what is to say he can't just hop a private diplomatic flight home ?"

"I will leave mine as well and I will also let you in on some pertinent information to the case; as soon as I get the proper permission."

"What information and what permission?" He asked softening.

"If you let me have the keys to Christian's apartment and allow me to talk to his boss. I will give you some new evidence."

"IF; and that is a very big IF; I do this I want one of my people to go with you."

"I would actually prefer that, since I am a little worried that the true arsonist may be looking for this information too."

"Fine then it is settled." the inspector pushed the button on his desk phone and in came a young plain clothed female police officer.

"Sir?" she asked expectantly.

"Madamesoille Ginger I would like you to meet Madamesoille Jeanna." They nodded at each other. The inspector continued, "Please escort her to the suspect's apartment." He looked at Ginger and said, "Don't let her out of your sight. Then I want you to take her to home of Monsieur Jolie."

"Oui Inspector Cordeaux." She said with a small salute and turned to Jeanna. "After you miss."

Jeanna headed out the office door and towards the main entrance. Ginger followed her to the door then stepped ahead, opened it and held it for her. She then headed down the stairs to a small car, Jeanna followed her and climbed in the passenger side door that Ginger was holding open

for her.

When they arrived at the apartment building Ginger handed Jeanna

the key, told her to unlock the front door and then follow her. Jeanna

unlocked the front door, stepped aside for Ginger and they headed down

the hall to his apartment. As they approached his door Ginger put her

hand out to stop Jeanna from continuing. Jeanna paused and noticed the

door slightly ajar, she waited as Ginger pulled out her weapon, then they

proceeded.

They moved forward cautiously and listened for noises from the

apartment. As they crept closer, they heard things being tossed about and

Ginger put her finger to her mouth and held her hand up signaling for

Jeanna to stop moving. Ginger approached the door and yelled "Alto!

Gandarme !" Jeanna heard a scuffle, a gunshot and then breaking glass.

She ran to the door with no thought of her own safety, only thinking of

Ginger. As she reached the door, she saw Ginger against the wall holding

her abdomen. Jeanna looked at her and Ginger pointed to the window, so

Jeanna used her cell phone to call the police department and told them

what happened, while she ran to the bathroom and grabbed towels to put on the wound. Ginger said she was okay and that it wasn't as bad as it looked. She told Jeanna to see if what she was looking for was still there.

Jeanna looked around, saw a photo that she had posed for Christian for. He had taken it when they just kids. It was such a goofy pose, she was even sticking out her tongue at him. She couldn't believe he still had it, he had told her it was one of the things he loved the most whenever she asked him why he kept it. She walked over to it, took it off the wall and looked behind it, but there was nothing there. Oh well it was a good try, she thought as she was about to put it back on the wall, then she felt something weird under the paper covering the back. She laid it on the table and saw a small slit, she ripped it open and saw a small micro SD card taped inside. She turned to Ginger and said, "I found it."

Ginger gave a pained grin and said, "Bon. Take my keys and go to his boss's house. The GPS in my car has the address typed in already."

Jeanna looked at her and asked, "Are you sure? Won't you get in trouble for letting me out of your sight?"

"I will explain to Inspector Cordeaux. Now go before you have to explain what happened here."

"Merci, Ginger. Keep pressure on it I hear them coming." Just then they both heard the sirens of the approaching police cars and ambulances. Jeanna rushed down the hall to the back stairs, she ran down them and then around to the side to where they had parked the car. She thanked the Goddesses that her Mom had insisted she learn to drive a European car and by European rules. She started the car, headed down the road and turned on the GPS. She put in the name of Christian's boss and up popped his address, she clicked on it and it gave her turn by turn directions to his house.

Chapter 6

As she was driving, she had time to think about her conversation with Christian and hated that he was right about how she really felt. She fiddled with the ring on her hand again and admitted it did feel right, but damn if she was about to tell him. After all he had left her, okay so he had good reasons, but he had hurt her badly when he left. Yes, he had tried to make it up to her, but he had still left her. She was so lost in thought she almost missed the turn for Monsieur Jolie's driveway.

She turned in quickly and pushed the button at the gate, she explained to the voice on the other end who she was and why she was there. The gate swung open, and she continued to drive up the driveway it felt like about a five mile. When she got to the end of it, she understood why, she saw a huge house the looked more like a castle.

As she got out of the car the front doors opened; a man she could only presume was the butler, stood holding them open til she got there. He told her to wait in the front hall area as he headed off towards a closed door, which she assumed was a library or den. A few moments later another man came out, she knew he had to be the owner of Chez Jolie, so she extended her hand and said, "Bon Soire Monsieur Jolie. I am Jeanna, Christian's friend."

"Oh yes Madamesoille Jeanna. He has spoken of you often and fondly. Please call me Jan. How can I help you?"

Jeanna's cheeks blushed at the knowledge that Christian had spoken of her. "Sir, Christian told me that he was looking into some missing inventory for you. He also told me he had found some information for you but didn't get a chance to give it to you before the arson happened. I have it here for you and I feel it may have something to do with the arson. I am hoping it can help clear him of the arson and thefts. I was hoping after you saw it you would allow me to give it to the police."

"You have it here?" He asked hopefully

"Yes. If you have a computer, I can show it to you now."

He led her to the door he had just walked out of and motioned to a laptop on his desk. As she sat down, she couldn't help but notice two distinctly different photos on his desk. One was a woman looking classically beautiful and elegant. The other was a woman who looked like she belonged on the cover of Vogue or Cosmopolitan. Jan noticed her staring and said, "That is my first wife, Janelle" pointing to the elegant woman, "She died of cancer 2 years ago." She saw the sadness in his eyes "And this is my new wife, Jasmine, she is a model." He didn't seem too pleased as he kind of spat out the word model with some disgust.

"They are both very beautiful." She said as she put the micro SD card in the reader slot of the laptop. She clicked on open all files and then a password box popped up. She looked at Jan and he shrugged his shoulders. She thought a minute and decided to give it a shot. She typed in her name and the screen said access granted. She blushed as she clicked on the file marked inventory and saw a video clip. She double-clicked it and they watched as an employee boxed up crab legs, lobster tails, jumbo shrimp, caviar and prime rib. Then he walked to the back door and opened it and let in another man. They chatted for a few minutes then the man who was let in handed the employee an envelope. The employee opened the envelope it was filled with money, he counted it, then handed the box to the man who then turned and left. She paused the video.

"Merde! Tu cochon! Tu fils de chienne!"

"Monsieur! I take it you know him?"

"Oui, it's my wife's worthless brother, Claude. I mean yes, he can cook, but he is such a spoiled brat. I had to hire him because he couldn't get a job anywhere else."

"He wouldn't by any chance be the other intern from Christian's school?"

"Oui, I only took him because no one else wanted him."

"There is more to this video should we watch more?"

"Oui." They started the video again and saw Claude walking out of the camera range and then returning. He had put a cigarette in his mouth and lit it with a match which he then tossed in a nearby bin, it was still red hot, then he walked out of the back door.

Jeanna and Jan continued to watch the bin in horror as it began to smoke and then burst into flames. "Merde! Sot!"

"What was in that bin?"

"That is where we put our rags that we use to oil/grease the pans with. That idiot knows that too."

"I am so sorry Jan, but at least now we know how it started and who did it. Now can we please give it to the police to try to help clear Christian?"

"Of course!" They stopped the video, ejected the SD card and she put it in her pocket. "I will follow you to the police station and we can straighten this out together."

"Great thank you so much." She couldn't help herself she hugged him. She pulled back almost instantly, and he let out a boisterous laugh.

"Let's go." They headed out of the room, to the main door and outside. "Oh merde, Jasmine has the car."

"That's fine I have this one we go in it if you trust my driving."

"I have heard about your driving from Christian. Maybe I should drive?"

"Really, he seems to have forgotten who got their license first, but you can drive." She handed him the keys and hopped into the passenger side of the car. Jan took the keys and hopped in the driver's seat and they

headed to the police station.

Chapter 7

As she walked into the police station the Sargent at the desk looked up and said, "So you came back."

"Of course. I told Ginger I would. By the way how is Ginger?"

"She's still in the hospital. She is okay though. She did tell us what happened. Inspector Cordeaux is waiting for you in his office."

She headed to the office and knocked on the door. "Entrez." Came from inside.

She walked in and saw Christian sitting in the chair. He stood up and turned to see her and Jan. "I see you found my evidence."

"Yes, we did, and Monsieur Jolie has agreed to let the police have it to help clear your name."

"Madamesoille, may I see this evidence?"

"Of course, here it is. You will see that there was more going on than just the arson. And that is wasn't really arson as much as it was a horrible stupidity." She walked to his laptop, put the SD card in the slot and double-clicked the file. As she put in the password, she was looking at Christian, he blushed and looked away. She opened the video and let the Inspector watch it all the way through.

He looked at her, Jan and Christian and said, "Okay so I see there is more here to investigate. I will release Christian now and drop all the charges. He is free to go." The three of them thanked him, left the office and headed for the door.

As they left the police station Jan looked at Christian and said "I am so sorry you had to go through this. I will do my best to make it up to you. What can I do, you name it?"

Christian looked at Jan, then back at Jeanna and said, "I am not sure I just need some time to think. I will get back in touch with you by tomorrow. Jeanna I will see you at the consulate later tonight I just need a walk to clear my head and get some fresh air."

Both Jeanna and Jan said goodbye to Christian and watched as he walked away. Jeanna was worried about Christian but wouldn't ever tell him. She knew he needed his space, so she offered Jan a ride back to his house, he said he was going to surprise Jasmine for dinner and let her know about her brother. So Jeanna headed back to the consulate to update

her mom with the news. And try to get some much-needed rest, it had

been a very long day and the jet lag was catching up to her.

Chapter 8

Later that evening, after unsuccessfully trying to sleep, Jeanna waited anxiously in the consulate lobby for Christian to appear. By 8pm Jeanna was so worried she figured she'd walked a hole in the floor, so she left word at the desk that she was going to his apartment to look for him.

She called for a consulate car and as she approached Christian's apartment, she felt an unnerving sense of dread. She jumped out of the cab, thanked the driver and ran up the four flights of stairs. She stopped short when she saw his door had been broken in. First thing she did was grab her cell phone to call the police and told them what she was seeing. The Sargent who took the call had been on duty when she had come in earlier, he immediately put her through to Inspector Cordeaux, and he dispatched some officers to her location. He told her to stay put, she said, "Over my dead body, Christian could be hurt or worse I'm not going to just wait." He told her to at least leave him on the line while she went to the door and looked around.

She agreed and left her phone active as got closer to the door and quietly peered in the opened door. She drew in a sharp breath as she saw blood on the floor. She carefully peered further into the room and saw two bodies on the floor. One was the worthless Claude and the other to her horror was Christian. She listened very carefully before she stepped into the room for any sign that someone else was there and when she was satisfied that no one was, she went inside. She relayed the scene to the inspector.

As she got closer, she saw the wound in Claude's chest, along with the lack of the chest rising and falling and knew immediately that he was dead. She looked around and saw a gun not far from Christian's body. She rushed to his side and checked for a pulse and wounds. She saw a black eye and noticed a bump on the back of his head. But thankfully he was alive, just unconscious. She again relayed the scene to the inspector who told her he was on his way with the forensics team.

Christian came to just as the police arrived with Inspector Cordeaux in the lead, the first things they saw were the dead body of Claude and the gun near Christian. They immediately did a GSR test on Christian which of course came back positive. So, they once again took him away to the station. Jeanna began to protest and tell them that it wasn't possible, there had to be an explanation, maybe Claude had broken in looking for the drive, then him and Christian fought over the gun and it went off. No one would listen to her theories, so she asked if she could look around. She pointed out she had on gloves and knew better than to move anything without informing the forensic guys. Inspector Cordeaux grumpily agreed, but insisted he stay and make sure she didn't bother his guys, so he had his men take Christian back to the police station.

Jeanna looked around she knew exactly what she needed; proof that someone fired a second shot with Christian's hand holding the gun to put the GSR on his hands, she knew the exact place to look too. She went to corner on a direct angle from Christian's body, she saw a potted plant and searched around it for a hole of some type, which she found. She called to Inspector Cordeaux and his techs and showed them the spot to examine. They found a spent round in the truck of the potted tree, which they marked and extracted. She also asked to have them check the round and said they may want to compare them to the one from earlier that day used to shoot Ginger. Another tech called the Inspector over and found a spent round casing under the couch near where Christian's body was. Jeanna got so excited she said, "Make sure you run it for prints."

Inspector Cordeaux looked at her exasperated and said, "Miss Jeanna I know you are concerned for your beau, but please realize we are not imbeciles here. We will do our jobs now, why don't you go back to the consulate, relax and let us."

Jeanna felt bad and said, "I am so sorry Inspector. I am just really worried about Christian. I know he didn't do it."

Jeanna called the consulate and had them send someone to the police station so they could examine Christian and see how old his injuries were; to determine if they were before or after Claude's shooting. She left word for her mother with the new development and then called her consulate car to take her for a drive to clear her head and try to relax.

Chapter 9

Jeanna left Christian's apartment, went to sit at the park from Christian's postcard and just stared at the train in absolute awe. It was so beautiful in real life that it took her breath away. However, what she saw next knocked it right back into her out of sheer shock. Across the park on the other side of the train sat a man who looked very familiar; she had watched his first movie only a few hours ago.

She grabbed her cell phone, turned on the video app and started recording his second. Hoping to get something that she could use to prove her theory that he was the real killer. She could at least show the video to Ginger and see if this man and the man who shot her were one in the same. Jeanna almost dropped the phone when she saw the sleek model looking woman approach him. She knew she had seen her somewhere before, but right now with her mind running in high gear, racing in a hundred directions she just couldn't place her. She just kept the camera aimed and going until they left. She got a great close video of the two of them parting with a kiss and tender embrace.

She debated following them, but when they hopped into a jaguar, she thought better of it and decided to head for the hospital where Ginger was instead. As she rode, she thought about the day she had had so far and was realizing she needed to get some rest before she dropped. She knew she should be heading to the consulate, but she also knew she had to show this video to Ginger.

She arrived a little after visiting hours but decided to try and see if she could talk to her for just a moment. She hoped that the nurse on duty was going to be nice as she was let off at the front door and headed inside.

Jeanna's wish must have been heard because it was answered, the nurse on duty said she would sneak her in since Ginger was so anxious to get out of there and wanted to see anyone any time. Jeanna paused at Ginger's door feeling bad she didn't have any gift for her, then she remembered the fan that had come in package that she had slid it into her purse. She pulled it out, hoped it would be good enough and that Ginger would like it.

As Jeanna entered the door Ginger turned from the TV, it was talking about the new development with the fire and how Christian was now back in custody for the murder of the arsonist. Jeanna just shook her head and said, "You can't believe everything you see on TV cause he wasn't really an arsonist; just a dork and Christian didn't do it."

Ginger smiled and said, "I know they never get the whole story before they air it."

Jeanna handed Ginger the fan and said, "I hope you like it."

"It's beautiful! I love it! I actually collect them, but don't tell anyone, I don't want them to know I have a girly side." Ginger said with a shy smile admiring the fan.

"Your secret is safe with me, I promise." Jeanna smiled at her "Can I ask you to look at a video I just took? I want to know if this is the same man who attacked you in Christian's apartment, this afternoon?"

"Sure, I got a kinda good look at him. It did happen fast, and he had a mask. I managed to remove it before he shot me though." Jeanna showed her the video she'd taken, and Ginger said, "Yeah that's the guy." As Jeanna went further through the video she paused on a good one with the woman and Ginger said, "Oh man that is not right in any way."

"What do you mean?" asked Jeanna

"Don't you know who that is?"

"I think so, but my mind isn't letting me grasp it."

"That's Madame Jolie." She said

"Oh man that's why she looked familiar. I saw her photo in the house when I went to see Monsieur Jolie. So why is she with this guy? He is the one her brother was selling the products to and he apparently is the one who ransacked Christian's apartment. So why is she making out with him?"

"Making out?" Ginger asked. Jeanna started the video again and paused at their tender goodbye kiss and embrace. "Man, that is so wrong. Poor Monsieur Jolie."

They looked at each other and said, "You don't think?" Ginger reached for her hospital phone and called headquarters. She told the Inspector what Jeanna had witnessed, about the video and that it was of the same man who had shot her. The Inspector said he would be right there to talk to them.

"Well I didn't want to sleep tonight anyway." Mumbled Jeanna as she sat on the chair to wait for Inspector Cordeaux.

"Jeanna go ahead and take a nap he has to come across town and the traffic is always bad. I promise I will wake you when he gets here." Ginger told her sympathetically. Jeanna smiled weakly curled up on the chair giving into her tiredness.

Chapter 10

Inspector Cordeaux arrived about an hour later and Ginger woke her up as he came in the door. They told him all about what her and Jeanna had discovered. He was skeptical at first, then Jeanna showed him the video. Inspector Cordeaux called his office and had them run a background check on Madame Jolie. They read him back what they found, and he talked to them a little more and then he had Jeanna send her video to his cyber tech's email and asked him to run the faces through the data base to see if anything popped.

When Cordeaux got the call back regarding what came back from the database and Madame Jolie's background check it was enough for him to tell his guys to release Christian and drive him to the embassy and drop him off. He just kept saying well I want them both in my office in 15 minutes, I don't care how you do it.

When he finally got off the phone Jeanna looked at him and asked, "What did you find out that made you let Christian go so quickly?"

"When we ran the photos from the video through the database, we got a hit on him and more on her. The information we got on her was interesting too. I'll fill you in on the way back to the station."

As Cordeaux drove, he told Jeanna about the information he had gotten. One piece really peaked her senses and that was that the new Madame Jolie had another name prior to marrying Monsieur Jolie than the one she told him, she also had a different face. Apparently, she had been a caregiver to other rich men's wives who had also died of their illnesses much quicker than expected. Then she had married them, and they had either died from some kind of violence, or mysteriously, or they had lost everything they had and then she had just disappeared.

This not only made her a murderess, but also a bigamist. The really bad part was that the man in the picture was not only her partner, but also her first legal husband, and they were still married. The only truth to her whole story was that the brother that was murdered was her real brother. Jeanna suggested they go to see Monsieur Jolie before heading back to the police station, just to make sure he was okay since they now knew Madame Jolie to be a "Black Widow". Inspector Cordeaux agreed with the idea and he turned down the next street so fast Jeanna was sure they were going to end up flipping the car.

They arrived at the Jolie's just in time to see a car speeding out of the driveway with Madame Jolie and her true husband in it. Jeanna said, "Let me out here I'll go check on Monsieur Jolie and you follow them."

"Oui", he said as he barely braked for Jeanna to jump out and rush to the house.

Jeanna ran to the house, saw the front door open and ran in. She saw the butler on the floor apparently unconscious, but she checked his vitals to be sure. To her relief she was right. She called the police headquarters and told them who she was and what was happening, then continued to search the house. She went to the bedroom first and found nothing, she then ran downstairs to the study and found Monsieur Jolie laying on the floor with a wound to his chest she rushed to him, placed pressure to the wound and was happy to hear him groan. She again called police headquarters she told them that she had found Monsieur Jolie and he need immediate attention, that he was bleeding from a chest wound and his pulse was weakening. They told her help was on the way and at the same moment she heard the sirens.

She heard footsteps and yelled that she was in the study. The medics arrived and took over she saw some officers she knew and asked if anyone had heard from Inspector Cordeaux. One told her that he had apprehended Madame Jolie and her accomplice after they had crashed into a tree trying to make a turn to fast. She asked if they were okay and the officer looked at her funny and said yes, she said "Good then they can stand trial for all their crimes."

Chapter 11

Monsieur Jolie was taken to the hospital and after a bit of touch and go the doctor said he would be fine, the bullet had missed his heart, but damaged his lungs. He was very lucky to be alive and as far as Monsieur Jolie was concerned, he owed his life to Jeanna. She told him no he owed it to Christian for sending her the mystery box that led her to France to start with. They agreed on that and he told Christian that if he wanted, he could have a permanent placement in his restaurant as a Head Chef. Christian thanked him but told him he was only trying to get training to go help his folks back home. But that he was planning on helping them train someone else to run the restaurant now since he realized he had to follow his real passion as a detective. Monsieur Jolie told him to have his folks contact him when he got home, that he had a business proposition for them. Christian told him he would.

Inspector Cordeaux met them at the hospital room and filled them in on what had happened and what Jasmine had confessed. She told them her brother was being paid to steal stuff for her true husband for his supper club. She claimed she was being forced by him to have Claude steal it. She said she had truly fallen in love with Jan, but that she said wanted him to lose his restaurant because he worked at it too many hours. She also said it upset her that it had been his and his first wife's passion, so she wanted him to give it up, so he could spend more time with her and forget the first Madame Jolie. She wanted to divorce Gerald; her real husband so that her marriage to Jan would be true. She claimed she had started out after the money, but then she had fallen in love with him for real. But when she found out he had not only used much of his money towards the restaurant, but also that he had donated much more for research into the cancer that had killed his wife, Jasmine got so angry she decided she would just make sure he couldn't use any more money. The truth was Jasmine had had a very short-lived career as a runway model and had not made much money and what she had made Gerald had taken for his supper club. So, she had gone to work as a caregiver for rich men. When she went to work for the first Madame Jolie. She fell in love with Jan and decided to hurry along her demise thinking she would not only get him, but also all his money.

What she didn't know was that even if she had managed to kill Jan, she wouldn't have gotten any money because he had never changed his will to include her getting anything. When Jeanna asked him why he hadn't changed it he told her that he was happy with his money going where it was and that he had never really even considered adding Jasmine to his will, because he didn't think she was interested in his money. He was going to leave her a place to stay and a small monthly payment to cover her bills, but the vast majority was staying the same.

Jeanna said "Well it would seem she tried to kill you for pretty much what she already had. Sad really." Everyone agreed, then they told Jan to rest and told him they would see him later. He thanked Jeanna again for saving his life, Christian for getting her there and the Inspector for the information.

As they left the Inspector complimented Jeanna on putting together the clues, information and even admitted she may have helped him solve the case. He even suggested she try to come to work for them. She thanked him but said she too had things to attend to in the states. He smiled thanked her again and said goodbye, handing them their passports.

Chapter 12

Jeanna and Christian headed back to the consulate to fill in her mother on what had happened and to make their arrangements to get back to the states. As they sat around the table for dinner the last 72 hours started to catch up to Jeanna and she was having a hard time keeping her eyes open. Apparently, the quick catnap in Ginger's hospital room hadn't helped at all. Christian noticed and said, "You look so tired Jeanna, you need to get some sleep before you collapse."

"I will. There is just one thing I can't figure out." She pulled out the ring she had stuffed in her pocket and said, "I figured out why you sent everything else in the box, except this. At first, I thought it was for me to get to see you, but since I have a consulate connection, I figured out that wasn't the reason. So why would you send this?"

Christian got up and walked to her chair. He dropped to one knee, Jeanna's mom gasped and Jeanna said, "So help me Christian if this is a dream or a sleep induced hallucination, I will kill you when I wake up."

Christian smiled and said, "No Jeanna, I am just waking from what seems to be a nightmare without you in my life. Please let my dream come true and say you'll marry me. Cause I love you and always have."

Jeanna just looked at Christian until her mom piped in and said, "Jeanna say something."

"Huh, UHM, you mean I'm not dreaming, and this is real?"

Christian and her mom laughed at her and both said "Yes this is real. Now what do you say?"

Jeanna smiled and said, "Of course I will, but you know I won't move to the city or here right. And my apartment is way too small for both of us. Where will we live?"

"Would you be okay with living in your old house?" He suggested hopefully.

"I know your father would want that." Her mom chimed in.

"And I was thinking we could make an office out of one of the downstairs rooms for our detective agency."

"Wait! What? Are you saying you want us to work together again?" She must be dreaming.

"Yes, if you want me?" He looked hopefully at her.

"Of course." Said Jeanna as the past 72 hours got the best of her and she literally passed out from exhaustion and fell off her chair.

Chapter 13

The next morning Jeanna woke up in her consulate bedroom dressed in her PJ's. She sat up right and looked around, she saw a small package and note on the small table by the window. She got up walked to the table sat at the chair and looked at the note while holding the package.

If you haven't changed you mind, please wear this ring and come talk to me. I really do love you and want to spend the rest of my life with you solving all kinds of mysteries. Including the most interesting one to me; you.

Love,

Christian

Jeanna opened the package and saw the ring that had come in the mysterious box. She smiled a small shy smile to herself, he could be so corny sometimes. She got up off the chair, walked to her closet and found one of her favorite outfits that she knew Christian used to love her in. She put on a light touch of makeup and sprayed a light mist of perfume he had given her years before. She pulled her hair back into a ponytail and headed out her bedroom door for the main stairs. She bound down them straight to her mom's office. Once there she knocked on the door and waited for her mom to tell her to come in.

After about ten minutes her mom yelled, "Come in sleepyhead."

Jeanna almost skipped into the room and said, "Well I probably needed it since I had been up over 72 hours. How long was I asleep anyways?"

"Oh only 36 hours."

"Wait... What? 36 hours? You are kidding me right. I slept over one entire day?"

"Yes, you did hunny. But we thought it best to let you rest since we knew how exhausted you were. Especially after you never even got a chance to recuperate from your first jet lag and now you are about to head back across again." Jeanna looked at her mom with bewilderment, that quickly turned to shock, then horror than utter depression. "Don't worry hunny he has just been getting things lined up with Jan to help out his folks back in the states."

"What do you mean?" asked Jeanna a lot confused. "And since when have you called Monsieur Jolie, Jan?"

Her mom blushed a little and said, "As far as Christian, Jan has agreed to help re-establish his family's restaurant in the U.S. By buying it and having them continue to run it. He is sending over some of his most promising students, who are also from the states; to help them get reset up and back on track. As well as updating the menu and some remodeling. Christian will help them oversee it when he has the time and report the progress back to Jan." Jeanna again raised an eyebrow at her mom using his first name. "As far as me and Jan he called to check on you the other night and to thank you again. We began talking and realized we had many things in common as well as having known each other for several months without realizing it. We have decided to begin spending some time together sharing our interest. I know how you feel..."

"Stop right there mom." Said Jeanna holding up her hand and walking closer to her mother. "I now realize that I was wrong about how I treated you regarding dad. I know it was him who told you to go and take this job and to not put your life on hold for him. I know that he didn't want either of us to give up our life for him. I just chose to do it for my own selfish reasons and you were strong enough to allow him to not have you see him as he was. I understand how hard it was for you to walk away and respect his wishes. I just wasn't ready to let him go and that was on me. I love you and I am happy that you have finally let yourself find someone who shares your interest. I am also happy that Monsieur Jolie isn't letting the crap his ex pulled stop him from searching for happiness. I hope you two have fun and can find happiness with each other. If not, I hope you both find happiness somewhere." Jeanna hugged her mother and said, "I really am happy for you and I love you."

Jeanna's mother started crying and said, "Thank you hunny I love you so much and I am so glad that you and Christian are getting back together." She nodded to the ring on her hand. "I know how hard it was on you when he moved here. I also know you felt like I abandoned you and your father when I took this job. I have never forgiven myself for that."

"Mom you know I can't lie about that, but I found a note from dad a little while ago. In it he explained to me about the talk you two had had and how he told you to take the job. He never wanted me to come home, but he knew he couldn't tell me that because I would've been upset. It took me a while, but I finally understand the he knew what was going to

happen and wanted to protect both of us from it. I was just way to

stubborn to let him."

"You are so much like him and he knew that. He called me when

you told him you were coming home, and he tried so hard to help you not

be angry. I told him to let you. It was better that you had someone to be

mad at and he should let you deal with in your own time. I knew one day

you would be willing to talk to me and let me back in."

Jeanna leaned to her mom and hugged her like she hadn't in a very

long time. She let all of her sadness she'd never faced out and just cried

and cried for what seemed like hours. As she finally got control of herself

and stood up, she felt Christian's arms around her, he was turning her to

face him. She buried her face in his shoulders, hugged him tightly and

cried some more for how badly she had treated him.

Christian just held her while she cried. He stroked her hair and

whispered "Let it out. It's okay, I'm here and I've got you. I'm never

gonna let you go again." Jeanna just held him tighter and continued to cry.

She had been so terrible, yet here he was holding and promising her forever. She knew she didn't deserve any of this and it made her cry

harder. She held him tighter and cried harder.

Chapter 14

Jeanna finally got control of herself and sat down on the couch next to Christian. Jan had come back with him to see her mom and he joined them. Christian and Jan told the ladies their ideas and plans for the restaurant and Jan told Jeanna's mom that he would need to go the states for a while to help Christian set it all up. Her mom said that was great she wanted to go back and help set up the house with Jeanna and prepare for the wedding. She called her assistant and told him about the upcoming trip and plans. He told her he would set up everything.

Christian had contacted his parents and they were so happy they said they would cater the wedding if Jan would be okay with that. He said of course it was a good chance for Christian to train his replacements in the restaurant. Jan had already told the students Christian had chosen to come to work there and they were thrilled. Jan had made arrangements for them to stay in a two-bedroom house he had rented in town, all expenses paid.

All the details were worked out, Jeanna and Christian went back to his apartment to pack up what he was taking on the plane. They had made arrangements to have trans-Atlantic movers come for the rest of his stuff

later in the week. Jeanna had let JB know about the new plans for extra

passengers to go back so him and Jan had gone to check out the storage

situation for not only the luggage, but for some special items Jan was

bringing back for Christian's parents.

Jeanna and Christian arrived at the airport in time to meet with her

mom and the students. They all entered the hanger together and saw Jan

next to a table with a small feast. He smiled and said, "This is a good way

to let our newest chefs see how our food should be presented. Plus, I think

the newly engaged couple deserves a small party, it is also my way to

show my appreciation for everything and they can also taste my ideas for

their wedding dinner." Everyone smiled, and they sat down to enjoy the

feast before the flight, even JB joined them, after he finished his pre-flight

checks. They all laughed and enjoyed the delicious food and general good

moods.

JB got up after a while and said, "Well if we want to get to the

States, I had better head for the cockpit and get us airborne." Everyone

agreed, and the four student chefs cleared the table and stowed the dishes

for cleaning when they landed. Everyone then took their seats just a JB announced over the cabin speaker that they were about to take off, so

everyone needed to buckle in. Jeanna sat next to Christian of course; her

mom sat next to Jan and the four student chefs sat in the back chatting

excitedly. Her mom and Jan talked in whispered tones and Jeanna just

leaned on Christian's shoulder still feeling tired from the last few days.

Christian just turned his head and kissed her forehead, as she fell asleep

for the duration of the flight.

Jeanna dreamed that her dad came to see her, and they talked about

everything that had just happened with her mom, her and Christian. He

told her he was happy for her mom and he hoped she would be too. He

was also glad that she had made up with her mom and Christian. He was

very happy that her and Christian were getting married and he hoped she

would now finally move back into the house and use it for her office and

he even suggested that Christian could cater a few small events just to

keep his skills honed. Plus, it would be useful if they ever had to

investigate someone who could be in need of catering. She smiled at him.

He kissed her forehead and told her he would always be watching over

her; how proud he was and how much he loved her.

Jeanna woke up as they touched down feeling much more confident about everything to come in the future from her new relationship to her new business and all the other changes. She smiled at Christian and said, "I am okay now. I know everything will work out and things will fall into place."

"How do you know that now?" He asked smiling at her.

"Let's just say I got some good advice from a trusted source." She smiled back and kissed him with all the love she had in her heart that she had been holding back all those years.

Made in the USA
Middletown, DE
29 July 2022